This LADYBIRD TALE
belongs to

....

The Princess and the Pea

Retold by Vera Southgate M.A., B.COM
with illustrations by Erica-Jane Waters

LADYBIRD 🐞 TALES

ONCE UPON A TIME there was a prince. When he grew up he wanted to marry a princess. But he wanted her to be a *real* princess.

The prince went all over the world looking for a *real* princess whom he could marry.

The prince met many princesses but there was always something the matter with them. One was too tall and another was too small. One was too sad and another was too jolly.

Somehow or other, not one of the princesses was just right. The prince was never quite sure if they were *real* princesses.

At last, the prince came home again. He was very sad because he did want to marry a *real* princess.

Then, one night there was
a terrible storm. The lightning
flashed, the thunder roared,
the wind blew and the rain
poured down.

In the middle of the storm there was a knock on the door of the castle. The old king went to open the door.

There, standing outside in the pouring rain, was a lovely lady. She might have been a princess, but she was so wet that it was difficult to tell.

Her hair was so wet that the water from it was running down her face. Her clothes were so wet that the water was pouring out of them.

Her shoes were so wet that the water was running in at the toes and out at the heels.

The king led the princess into the castle, out of the wind and the rain.

There she stood, in a pool of water, and all she could say was, "I am a *real* princess."

The prince could not believe
his ears when he heard her say,
"I am a *real* princess."

"We'll see about that," thought
the old queen, but she did not
say anything.

While the princess was being bathed and dried and dressed in dry clothes, the queen went to see about a bedroom for her.

The queen had all the bedclothes taken off the bed. Then she put a pea under the mattress.

Then, more and more mattresses were put on top, until there were twenty mattresses on top of the pea.

Then the queen had twenty
feather beds piled on top of the
twenty mattresses.

"Now we shall find out if you
are a *real* princess," said the
queen to herself.

When the princess was warmed
and fed, the queen led her to the
bedroom and tucked her into bed.

In the morning, the old queen
went to see the princess.

"How did you sleep, my dear?"
she asked her.

"Dreadfully," replied the princess, "I hardly slept a wink all night!"

"What was the matter?" asked the old queen.

"I do not know what was in the bed," replied the princess, "but there was something hard in it. Now I am black and blue all over."

Then the queen knew that
this was a *real* princess because
she had felt the pea through
twenty mattresses and twenty
feather beds. Only a *real* princess
could be as tender as that.

The prince was filled with joy
when the old queen told him
that they had indeed found
a *real* princess.

A wedding was arranged between the prince and the *real* princess. Then there was great joy in the castle.

As for the pea, it was placed in
a museum. It may still be seen
there – if no one has taken
it away!

A History of
The Princess and the Pea

One of Hans Christian Andersen's best-known stories, *The Princess and the Pea* has inspired books, musicals, plays and even ballets.

This short story appeared in Andersen's first collection of tales for children in 1835, *Eventyr, fortalte for Børn* (*Tales, Told for Children*). It quickly became a popular story, depicting a prince's search for the perfect princess bride.

The fairy tale gained wide popularity in 1960 with the musical adaptation, *Once Upon a Mattress*. Since then, other dramatic versions have been produced for radio, television and the stage.

All of these versions feature a princess
who is seeking refuge in a castle,
a queen determined to find out if
the girl is a true princess and,
of course, twenty mattresses and
twenty feather beds!

Ladybird's 1967 retelling, told by
Vera Southgate, is a classic of its
time and helped to bring the story
to a new generation.

Collect more fantastic
LADYBIRD 🐞 TALES

Little Red Riding Hood

9781409311126

Goldilocks and the Three Bears

9781409311119

Cinderella

9781409311072

Jack and the Beanstalk

9781409311102

The Gingerbread Man

9781409311096

The Three Little Pigs

9781409311089

The Three Billy Goats Gruff

9781409311065

Hansel and Gretel

9781409311133

Puss in Boots

9781409311225

Rapunzel

9781409311195

Rumpelstiltskin

9781409311164

The Elves and the Shoemaker

9781409311188

Snow White and the Seven Dwarfs	The Enormous Turnip	The Magic Porridge Pot
9781409311171	9781409311218	9781409311201

Sleeping Beauty	The Princess and the Frog	Dick Whittington
9781409311157	9780718192556	9780718192532

The Big Pancake	Beauty and the Beast	The Little Red Hen
9780718192549	9780718192587	9780718192525

The Ugly Duckling	The Princess and the Pea	Chicken Licken
9780718193133	9780718192570	9780718192563

Endpapers taken from series 606d,
first published in 1964

A catalogue record for this book is available from the British Library

Published by Ladybird Books Ltd
80 Strand London WC2R 0RL
A Penguin Company

001

© Ladybird Books Ltd MMXIII

LADYBIRD and the device of a Ladybird are trademarks of Ladybird Books Ltd

ISBN: 978-0-71819-257-0

Printed in China